THIS BOOK BELONGS TO:

_____

For Chris Stephenson, for all your kind words. J.W.

This paperback edition first published in 2012 by Andersen Press Ltd.
First published in Great Britain in 2010 by Andersen Press Ltd.,
20 Vauxhall Bridge Road, London SW1V 2SA.
Published in Australia by Random House Australia Pty., Level 3,
100 Pacific Highway, North Sydney, NSW 2060.
Text copyright © Jeanne Willis, 2010
Illustration copyright © Tony Ross, 2010
The rights of Jeanne Willis and Tony Ross to be identified as the author and
illustrator of this work have been asserted by them in accordance with the
Copyright, Designs and Patents Act, 1988.

Colour separated in Switzerland by Photolitho AG, Zürich.
Printed and bound in Singapore by Tien Wah Press.

10   9   8   7   6   5   4   3   2

British Library Cataloguing in Publication Data available.

ISBN 978 1 84939 025 5

This book has been printed on acid-free paper

Caterpillar Dreams

Jeanne Willis and Tony Ross

ANDERSEN PRESS

It was dawn. A soft breeze blew.
In the wild grass, two flowers danced.

They didn't look the same.
They didn't dance the same.
But they danced for the same reason.

They both had a secret.
It was hidden in their leaves.
The secret would soon be out.

Eggs! Mysterious eggs.
Not snails. Not frogs . . .

Caterpillars!

Two curly caterpillars.
One stripy. One plain.

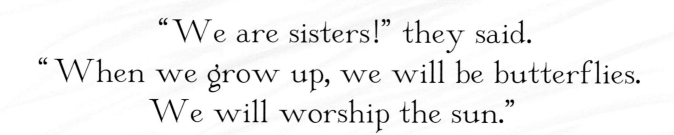

"We are sisters!" they said.
"When we grow up, we will be butterflies.
We will worship the sun."

Day by day they grew.

By night, they dreamed of all the things
they would do, when they were butterflies.

They would wake to the song of the blackbird.
And fly through skies of forget-me-not blue.

They would sip from buttercups...

flit through sunbeams...

and bathe in gold dust.

The days grew long.
The caterpillars grew longer.
"It won't be long now," they said.
"We will be butterflies. Beautiful butterflies.
Sisters under the sun."

The bees were leaving.
The flowers turned to seed.

"When the sun sleeps, we will sleep," the caterpillars said.
"When we wake, our dreams will all come true."

The bees left. The flowers fell.
The sun went down.
Just as the caterpillars hoped.

But Nature had her own hopes.
Her own dreams.

Which were not the same as theirs.

The sun came up.
The first sister woke.

But she was alone.

She flew through skies of forget-me-not blue.
She searched among the sunbeams.
But her sister wasn't there.

The sun set. A nightingale sang.
Lullaby Butterfly.
The butterfly slept.

In her dream, she saw her sister.
She had woken to the owl.
She was worshipping the moon.

Soaring through space.

Skipping through moonbeams.
Bathing in stardust.

Dawn came. Where dark meets day, they met.

One was a moth and one was a butterfly.

Different dreams, but just as beautiful.

We cannot all be butterflies it seems.
The world needs moths just like it needs the moon.

That's what keeps it turning, turning, turning.
Same lullaby. It's just a different tune.

Sweet dreams.

Other books by
JEANNE WILLIS AND TONY ROSS:

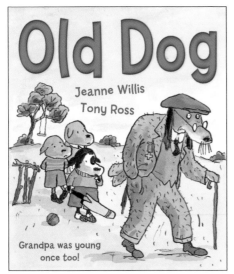

9781842708804

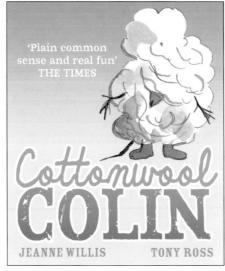

9781842707197

9781849392167

9781842705711

9781842707579

Mayfly Day

9781842706060